Pucking Human

Thin Ice #7

Charity Parkerson

Punk & Sissy Publications

Copyright

—Warning: This book is intended for readers over the age of 18. Some of my books contain allusions to past abuse and trauma.

Editor: BZ Hercules & Consultants

CONTENTS

Introduction	1
Chapter One	3
Chapter Two	18
Chapter Three	33
Chapter Four	53
Chapter Five	69
Chapter Six	84
Chapter Seven	94
Chapter Eight	115

Chapter Nine 131
Chapter Ten 160
About the Author 186

Introduction

Some days, Rider is a terrible boss. Other days, he's a dream. Either way, he's completely off limits.

After a long and successful hockey career, Rider moved on to take over the general manager position of a professional hockey team. It's not exactly the cozy job he hoped it would be. In fact, he might be out on his butt soon if he can't win a championship. But the job still has its perks—like a sassy personal assistant who couldn't be deeper beneath Rider's skin.

Rider is rich, spoiled, and maddening. The guy is barely human. He drives Ben insane with his arrogant ways. Despite all those things, Ben has no desire to be anywhere else. His long working hours are the happiest of his day. The fire between them seems like so much more than friction. They have a spark. Zero good can come of a workplace romance, especially when Rider has nothing to gain, and Ben has everything to lose.

Pucking Human is the seventh book in Charity Parkerson's Thin Ice series. These books are steamy sports romances meant to heat up your day. This series is best enjoyed when read in order.

Chapter One

The Tuesday night crowd was every bit as enthusiastic as the Saturday crowd. It helped that the Chuckers were headed straight toward a ship. Rider watched from the owner's box, the way he did at every home game. He chewed antacids like they were candy. Everything rode on this season. If the team's owner, Tanner Paige, kicked him to the curb, financially, Rider would be fine. Not only had he come from a long line of professional athletes, he had played pro hockey for twelve years before getting this job. But if Tanner booted him from the sport, then that was what would happen. He would lose his only connection to his greatest love: the game.

“Give me those. If you keep this up, you’ll never shit again.” Ben swiped the antacids from Rider’s hands.

Ugly words rose in Rider’s throat. He bit back the desire to lay into the bossy assistant. He hated when Ben scolded him, especially when they weren’t alone.

Ben handed him a prescription bottle. “If you’d take the right meds, you wouldn’t need these.” He shook the fruity flavored over-the-counter meds at him.

Rider rolled his eyes and twisted the lid from his prescription. Before he tossed back the pill, Ben took the bottle from him and handed him an open bottle of water.

"Don't take that dry. It won't help. Plus, I don't want to perform the Heimlich tonight."

"Remind me to fire you tomorrow." Rider mumbled the threat under his breath. He never won arguments against Ben.

Ben's gorgeous hazel eyes sparkled with challenge. "What was that?"

Rider swallowed the pill with a healthy dose of water before responding. "Thank you."

Ben hummed. It was an oddly sexy sound. "That's what I thought."

The crowd roared as a buzzer sounded. Another win. Rider went back to watching the ice. Lev Medvedkov took his victory lap. Every time the guy showed up and showed out, Rider breathed another sigh of relief. He had taken a huge gamble by paying the guy more than he had ever paid for another player. Tanner hadn't exactly balked, but he also made sure Rider understood the decision was on his head.

Ben leaned his way, bumping shoulders with him. "There. You can breathe again until Saturday."

Rider met Ben's stare. They shared a smile. Rider opened his mouth, hoping to convince Ben to stay late with him. A slap across his back pulled Rider's attention to the man, who approached to congratulate him.

"Great job, Rider. Genius move getting Medvedkov and Coach Murphy this year. Fucking magic."

Rider smiled and dipped his chin, accepting the compliment. "I live for this team." It was the way Rider always responded. In truth, landing Medvedkov hadn't been his doing as much as it was Murphy's. Lev and Murphy had fallen in love. Rider had taken advantage of their feelings to lure Medvedkov to stay in New Orleans. It had been more manipulative than genius. Still, Rider took his congratulations from the room of businessmen and celebrities who took advantage of the owner's box. He couldn't ignore them. Players weren't the only way they made money. Sponsorships were every bit as important as winning. Rider had to keep people wanting to add their names to the arena during games.

By the time Rider finished rubbing elbows, he turned in time to catch Ben slipping out the door. Disappointment washed over him. Ben wasn't required to stay past game time. Rider knew he could call and Ben would come back, but he didn't have any legitimate excuse for that. Still, Rider followed. He didn't intend to stop him. Rider only wanted to make sure Ben made it to his car unaccosted. Ben had a huge personality, but he was a small guy. He still turned heads. His perfectly styled dark hair and sexy round ass made people look twice. Those things also held Rider's attention. It was more than looks, though. Ben made Rider feel alive. Things had been this way since Rider hired him two years ago. His obsession hadn't started right away. That had grown over time, getting bigger every day. The way Ben's eyes sparkled with challenge kept Rider on his toes. Rider couldn't get enough.

Ben stepped into the elevator and turned. Their gazes met. An evil-looking smile touched Ben's lips. He pressed the button to close the doors faster. As it slid closed, a soft chuckle fell from Rider's lips. He was such an asshole. Rider couldn't get enough.

Ben's cheeks hurt from smiling. The ride to the ground floor took forever. It stopped on every floor. He hadn't considered everyone else leaving the game. Ben had run from Rider. Everything about the guy was a challenge. Ben loved it. Every other aspect of his life was boring and empty as hell. Tonight, Rider had driven him insane with the constant popping of antacids. Geez. The guy had a fucking prescription for ulcers. Without Ben, he would be in the ER right now, hoping for relief. Since they had made it through the night without ending in a screaming match, Ben had darted out the first chance he had gotten. Sometimes he had to take his wins and go. Rider had been in one of those moods. Ben knew how to read him after two years of being his personal assistant. He knew when to cut and run.

The elevator reached the ground floor. Ben didn't get off when the doors opened. Instead, he hesitated. Then he watched himself insert his key to get back to the executive floor. It was out of his control. Ben told himself he needed the jacket he had left in the office. Despite spring's arrival, the nights were still slightly chilly. Somewhat. Maybe enough for a light jacket.

Knots tightened in his stomach as the elevator took him back upstairs. Rider thought he had left. He could be up to anything by now. Up for anyone. They spent most of their time together. Ben knew Rider wasn't celibate. He spent a ridiculous amount of time praying he never actually saw Rider with anyone else. It had been a year and a half since he had been forced to endure watching Rider leave the office with someone else. Occasionally, Ben was tasked with sending flowers or wine to some unknown person. It had been at least six months since he had been asked to do that. Ben lived in fear of doing it again.

As he neared the top floor, Ben almost changed his mind. This job was all he had. If Rider had found his fun for the night, Ben might quit. Honestly, he had no idea how he would react. He pressed his hand to his stomach, trying to hold in the fear. When the doors opened, Ben stepped out into the quiet hallway leading to the corporate offices. The nights were always nice here. No phones rang. Peace filled the air.

Light spilled from the open doorway of the office he shared with Rider. Ben's nerves frayed. He almost turned around. What if Rider was inside with someone? Ben's steps slowed as he approached the door. He froze and listened. No sound emerged from the room. He chanced a quick peek around the corner. Rider sat at his desk alone, staring at nothing as if lost in thought. Ben stepped into the room.

Rider's ice-blue gaze turned his way. Ben's heart skipped a beat. Rider's hard features didn't soften. They rarely did. His dark hair grayed at the edges. Forty-one looked damn good on him.

Ben smiled. "Sorry. I didn't know you were still here." He motioned toward his desk in the corner of Rider's office. "I forgot my jacket."

Leaned back in his chair with his dress shirt sleeves rolled up to his elbows, Rider linked his fingers behind his head and stretched. The move made his shirt strain against the huge muscles he had built from years of playing professional hockey. As always, the sight mesmerized Ben. A tired, sexy-looking grin flashed across Rider's face. "I haven't checked the weather. Is it cold out there?"

Ben shrugged. "I didn't make it outside. You never know this time of year. If it's warm tonight, it's likely to be freezing in the morning or vice versa."

"True." Rider picked up his phone as if dismissing Ben.

Ben headed for the jacket hanging on the back of his chair.

"It's fifty-four degrees, according to my phone."

"Oh." Ben grabbed his jacket. "It's a good thing I came back, then."

"Fifty-four isn't cold."

A laugh burst from Ben at Rider's comment. "Maybe for you. Some of us don't have your thick body." Fuck. Had he just said that?

"Did you just call me fat?"

Ben shot him an exasperated look. "Spare me. You know I didn't."

The evil smile Rider wore let him know Rider was just fucking with him.

Ben rolled his eyes. "I'll see you tomorrow." He headed for the door.

"Ben."

Ben froze and turned back Rider's way. "Be safe going home."

Ben dipped his chin. "You too." He turned away and took two steps.

"Ben."

He fought a huff as he turned around again.

"Text me when you get there, so I know you made it."

With an eye roll, he headed for the door again. He got one foot into the hallway.

"Ben."

He growled. His gaze moved back to hold Rider's stare.

Rider smiled like an idiot. "How far would you have made it if I hadn't called you back?"

God, Rider drove him crazy. "Ass."

"Pfft. You love me."

Ben shook his head and walked away before his stupid heart gave away his thoughts. Sometimes, deep down in a secret place no one could see, Ben very much feared he did love Rider. That was the scariest part of all.

Chapter Two

He smelled good today. So fucking good. Ben had to stay at his desk to keep from sniffing him. The temptation to ask if Rider got a new cologne was killing him. Fuck. He smelled delicious. Unfortunately, for whatever reason, Rider's mood was complete shit. He had already barked at Ben twice. His face was twice as hard as usual, and Ben knew him well enough to keep his mouth shut. Rider didn't get like this often, but it was always bad when he did.

“Where in the fuck are this week’s stat sheets?”

Ben bit back a tired sigh. “In the file on your computer, clearly labeled as stat sheets.”

Rider shot him an irritated look. “No fucking shit, Ben. The file is missing. Did you think I asked because I have nothing better to do?”

After a calming breath, Ben moved to his feet and crossed the room. He leaned over Rider’s shoulder. That smell hit him square in the face. He fought his eyes from slipping closed. Damn. He wanted to wallow in that scent. Instead, he used Rider’s mouse to click around. He opened the file finder and searched stats, finding Rider's lost file. Ben opened it and walked away before he rubbed himself against Rider like a cat.

"How in the fuck did it end up in the cloud?"

"It's always in the cloud," Ben said, trying to hold on to his patience. "That's how you're able to access it from any device."

"I'm detecting a tone."

Ben met his stare.

Rider's eyes were narrowed.

It seemed they would be fighting today. "What tone would that be?"

"A snippy one."

Ben's eye twitched. "You're hearing things." Now he sounded snippy.

"I don't think I am." Damn. Rider sounded pissed.

"I'm guessing now isn't a good time to tell you to calm down."

The muscle in Rider's jaw ticked. "Are you trying to get fired?"

Ben ran his tongue over his teeth. Rider obviously needed to have it out with someone. That was fine. Ben had time. "Do you want to fire me? Fine." He pointed at the nearby thousand-dollar coffee station. "Go right over there and show me step by step how your coffee is made." Ben swiped his hand through the air. "Scratch that. That one is way too hard. Let's try an easier one, since I'm so disposable to you. Tell me where your car keys are right this second. Go on. I'll wait."

They held each other's stare.

Neither of them blinked.

Finally, an adorable and contrite smile touched Rider's lips. He leaned back in his chair and ran his hands through his hair, making it stand on end. Rider flattened it out again. "Sorry. I talked to my mom this morning."

Ben winced. Rider's mom, Jules, was the fucking worst. She was spoiled and high maintenance, even though she had done nothing to deserve it. After marrying a professional football player, she had produced three sons who all grew up to play various pro sports. She fully expected to be regularly compensated for giving them life. That was all she had done. Nannies had raised them.

"What new toy has she decided she wants your dad won't buy her now?"

"A twenty-three-year-old pool boy named Stephan."

An unexpected laugh burst from Ben. He covered his mouth. "Sorry."

Rider shook his head. His smile was everything. "Don't be. It's fucking ridiculous. Apparently, Dad fired the equestrian trainer she was sleeping with, but he refused to get rid of the tennis instructor he's fucking. So now she wants a full-time pool guy he won't fund." Rider swiped a hand over his face. "It's all so goddamn dumb."

"Why don't they just get divorced?"

Rider shot him a look like he thought Ben was an idiot.

Ben nodded. “Right. No one is willing to split the assets.”

“Bingo.” Rider straightened in his seat and eyed his desk as if he had forgotten what he had been doing. After a moment, he sighed and met Ben’s stare again. “Let’s get out of here for a few hours.”

Ben shrugged. “Okay.” If it meant Rider’s mood improved, he would do anything. He despised Rider’s parents for just this reason. Rider lived under constant pressure. He already had ulcers and didn’t sleep. The last thing he needed was more people crushing him with impossible expectations. Ben opened the top drawer of his desk and grabbed Rider’s keys.

Rider laughed at the sight of them. “Where did you find them this time?”

"They were on the floor in the bathroom."

With a shake of his head, Rider stood. "I honestly couldn't live without you."

Ben didn't bother hiding his bright smile. "I know." Together, they headed out while Ben did a happy dance inside. He had made Rider laugh. His day was complete.

Rider hadn't just been talking shit. He genuinely couldn't live without Ben. The guy ran his entire life, keeping him on track and picking up every place Rider lacked. Stress made him forgetful as hell and he lost everything all the time. Ben never hesitated to go toe to toe with him when he was being an ass. Honestly, that was exactly what he needed. Someone weak could never survive him. Ben's bravado always snapped Rider from his bad moods.

For that, Ben deserved a nice day away from the office. They went to lunch at Ben's favorite restaurant. Rider could take it or leave it. It was one of those too busy places that anchored every mall. The food was just all right, in Rider's opinion, but he had been raised completely different than Ben. Ben saw the place as overpriced and nice. For Rider, it was kind of blah. But it was attached to an upscale mall, which gave Rider an excuse to take Ben shopping. Unlike his undeserving and ungrateful mother, Ben deserved nice things. Rider loved spoiling him because Ben fucking hated it. Every gift made him visibly uncomfortable. Rider enjoyed watching him squirm.

"Which store should we hit first?"

Ben shot him a laughing look. He tapped his chin. Rider couldn't wait to hear what sassy thing he intended to say. Ben surprised him. "Show me where you bought this new cologne. I'm in love."

Hunger unexpectedly punched Rider in the gut. Until that moment, he hadn't realized how badly he wanted to hear that L word roll from Ben's tongue. Plus, he had admitted to liking Rider's scent. That felt like a win.

"As you wish." He grabbed Ben's hand and tucked it into the crook of his arm, being the gentleman. “This way, my good man.”

Ben chuckled at his ridiculousness, but he didn’t pull away. As they headed inside a high-end department store, Ben laughed again. “I honestly thought you’d tell me some exotic lover gave you the cologne. You’re not someone I picture out shopping for something like that... at the mall.”

Rider shot Ben an irritated look. “Don’t be ridiculous. You, of all people, should know I don’t date.”

Ben didn’t meet his stare. His gaze swept the store, taking in every detail. “Why is that? Anyone would be lucky to have you, and I know people trip over themselves to win you.”

You. The reason is you. That thought was so loud, he worried he might have said the words aloud, but Ben didn't react. Rider assumed he managed to keep his trap shut. "Who has time for that bull-shit?"

Finally, Ben's gaze swung his way. Their gazes collided. He swore something built between them. Ben looked away first. "You had time to go cologne shopping. That means you have time to date."

"I had to come here for a different reason. The cologne was an afterthought."

"Nice afterthought. Then again, you've always had good taste. After all, you hired me."

"Best decision I ever made."

They exchanged a smile.

Ben squeezed his arm. "So what were you out shopping for when you had this afterthought? I'm genuinely curious now."

Rider shrugged. "Someone I know has a birthday and a two-year anniversary of working for me next week."

A loud and obnoxious gasp burst from Ben. "Who? Is it Cynthia in accounting?"

Rider laughed. Ben was one of a kind. "Does she have a birthday next week? How sad for you, having to share your day with someone else."

Ben chuckled. "I'm sure I share my day with millions around the world."

"Yet there's only one you," Rider said, trying to keep the mood light. "Now, you are notoriously hard to buy for, so what would you like?"

Ben huffed. It was an adorable sound. "You didn't even buy me anything? I'm joking, of course. Please don't buy me anything."

"A surprise it shall be." He slung his arm across Ben's shoulders and steered him toward the shoe section. "For funsies. Let's get you some new shoes. The ones you're wearing are terrible."

Ben laughed. It was genuine and turned heads.

Rider couldn't look away.

"You bought me these shoes."

"But they're so last year," Rider argued.

"You bought them two months ago."

Rider played dumb. “Did I? I don’t think that’s right. Either way, two months is too long.”

Ben shook his head. “You’re impossible.”

Rider’s face hurt from smiling. All the stress fell away, leaving him feeling free. He only felt this way with Ben. Rider said what he always did whenever Ben complained about him. “Don’t fuss. You love me.”

Ben flashed him an exasperated look. One of these days, Ben would agree. Rider lived for that day.

Chapter Three

It had been the best day. Ben had eaten so much, he thought he might pop. Rider had bought him seven new outfits, claiming they were a business expense. No matter how hard Ben argued, Rider wouldn't be denied. Secretly, Ben loved it. Without Rider, he would never have new clothes, much less clothes this expensive. While he made good money working for Rider, life kept getting more expensive every day, and his debt kept growing. Ben couldn't afford to be frivolous.

Rider helped him carry bags inside his apartment. One thing Ben adored about Rider was how Rider never made him feel uncomfortable about their difference in wealth. Ben knew Rider had been raised drowning in money. He knew Rider had to be horrified by the idea of apartment living and not owning a car. Having to walk through homeless people to get inside. Rider never batted an eye. It had taken Ben a little while to believe it wasn't an act. After two years, Ben accepted Rider didn't look down on him. It was one of the many reasons Ben had tolerated Rider's demanding and sometimes abrasive personality.

"Thank you again for all this," Ben said, dumping the bags on the couch. "Now, don't show up next Tuesday with a birthday gift. You've bought me enough."

"Show up next Tuesday with a birthday gift. Got it."

Ben sighed.

Rider smiled innocently.

How could Ben resist falling in love with him? That thought had a lump swelling in Ben's throat. One day, Rider would meet someone and get married. Ben would have to watch it happen in silence.

He cleared his throat. "Can I get you something to drink?"

Rider eyed him. "Are you okay?"

Ben forced a smile to his lips. "Of course. It just hit me how much work we'll have tomorrow after skipping out today."

"Well, how much work you'll have," Rider reminded him with a laugh. "I don't actually have to do much at all. Thanks to an amazing assistant, of course." Rider's phone rang. He checked the face. "Jesus Christ. It's Mom again. Just give me a second and I'll take that drink."

Ben nodded. He grabbed the bags and headed for his bedroom. After dropping everything on the bed, he trudged back to the kitchen to see if he had anything Rider would drink. No noise came from the living room. Ben checked to see if Rider had disappeared. He sat on the couch, staring at nothing.

"That was fast."

Rider's gaze moved Ben's way. He cleared his throat. "My father passed away."

Ben drew a sharp breath, as if he had been punched in the chest. While Rider had a contentious relationship with his mom, and he disapproved of many of his father's life choices, Rider very much loved his dad. Despite his fame, he had been a hands-on father. He had trained his sons to capture the same level of stardom he had achieved, while also assuring them it didn't matter if they failed. He would love them anyhow. Ben was a bit jealous of that.

Despite the loss having nothing to do with him, Ben's eyes stung. He had to blink to keep from crying. "Are you okay? Never mind. That's a stupid question. What can I do?"

Rider made a helpless gesture.

Ben nodded. He got it. Rider needed what he always needed from Ben: for Ben to handle his life. “Okay. We’ll go to your place and pack your things. We’ll have to stop by the office to get your passport and I’ll charter you a flight. I’ll drive.” He held Rider’s stare. “Don’t worry. I’ll take care of everything.”

Rider made a jerky sort of nod Ben assumed was an agreement. Ben patted Rider’s pockets, looking for his keys. Rider touched his arm, stopping him. “Go pack, okay?”

Ben didn’t argue. It wasn’t unusual for Rider to demand his presence on business trips. Rider was the reason Ben even had a passport. He had never needed one before Rider took him to get one, intent on Ben being wherever he was needed. Ben headed for his room and packed.

Both their passports were in a safe in Rider's office, ensuring they could drop everything and go at any second. The team's owner lived in Canada. It wasn't unusual for him to demand an in-person meeting at the last minute, expecting a trip to a whole other country should be like a leisurely stroll down the street. That one was a rich one out of touch with reality. Ben had learned to adjust. All those panicked races across the country had prepared Ben for tonight. He knew exactly how to get them to Puerto Vallarta in a hurry. Ben would do what he could. It felt like not enough, but nothing was enough in a situation like this. He had to be Rider's rock.

Nothing felt real. Rider felt numb. Ben buzzed around him, handling everything like the professional he was. Meanwhile, Rider had nothing. He didn't know what to say or how to act. Part of him expected to get to Mexico and learn his mom was only being dramatic. She had never gone as far as this, but she could be a little crazy when she didn't get her way.

Unfortunately, no. The minute Ben drove their rental into his parents' driveway, he knew that hope was a fantasy. His brothers were already there. Ben grabbed their bags and followed him to the door. Rider knew he should help, but he couldn't feel his arms. Everything felt like walking through a dream. A nightmare.

As he stepped inside, the silence was deafening. It was as if everyone walked on their toes and held their breath. He found everyone in the living room not saying a word. His mom looked up as he stepped into the room. Her eyes were red-rimmed and bloodshot from crying. At the sight of him, she immediately fell into hysterics. That was the way of things in their family. He was the oldest. Rider was the one she always called when things went wrong. Her other sons were her babies. He was the one who carried the load—like a third parent.

Rider did what was expected of him. He sat next to his mom and comforted her. She started rambling. "I don't know what happened. One second, we were arguing and then he told me to call nine one one.

I thought he was being funny." She cried harder.

Rider patted her and stared at nothing. Inside, he fell apart, and no one noticed. His gaze moved to the doorway where Ben still stood, looking out of place. His gaze was locked on Rider. One person knew. The sympathy in Ben's eyes nearly broke him. Ben saw him like no one else. He saw beneath the rigid demeanor. Rider wanted to be alone with him. He needed Ben to let him rage.

His mom noticed Ben. She stopped wailing. Her voice changed, like nothing happened. "Oh. Jacob will show you where to take those." She spoke as if dismissing a servant. In fact, Jacob was her butler. Irritation flashed through Rider, but Ben simply nodded. Jacob appeared at his side and whisked him away, as if hiding the help. Rider took a calming breath. He needed to be strong. They had planning to do. As always, Matt and Harlan would be useless. Everything would fall to him. Rider fought an irrational desire to laugh. If they only knew. Rider didn't even know where his keys were. Ben ran his life. Rider didn't know how to do this.

It wasn't the least bit unusual for Ben to get delegated to hanging out with the household staff. That's how he was seen. When they went to Canada for meetings with Tanner, Ben always went to the kitchen and waited for the inevitable moment Rider would call him into the room.

Rider didn't run the Chuckers alone. Ben kept him organized.

This was different. Rider's family didn't need him. Ben stayed in his place. The kitchen staff saw him as a guest but tolerated his presence. They served him the way they did the family, but they didn't speak freely. Everyone worked quietly, as if Ben conducted a performance review. He drank tea and fretted. Jacob had put Ben in the room next to Rider's, but Ben couldn't go to bed until he saw Rider one last time for the night. He had looked so lost while comforting his mother. Ben had wanted to run to his side. Instead, he was here, getting odd looks from people who wanted him out of their kitchen.

The third time the chef shot him an annoyed look, Ben stood. He worried he might be keeping them from going to bed. It hadn't occurred to him they couldn't leave until they knew the family no longer needed anything.

"If you don't mind, I'll take a cup of tea to Rider, then head to bed."

The guy nodded and poured a cup. Ben doctored it to Rider's liking and then headed for the living room. To his surprise, everyone still sat where he had left them, as if three hours hadn't passed, and it wasn't one in the morning.

Rider's gaze swung Ben's way as Ben entered the room. His eyes looked dead. Ben headed his way. He held out the cup. "You should drink this. Do you need anything else before I go to bed?" He felt the eyes upon him. Ben didn't care. He was there for Rider.

Jules spoke up before Rider answered. "Oh. Tea sounds lovely. Grab a tray for everyone. Maybe some cookies too."

"He isn't a servant." Rider sounded more tired than angry.

Ben needed to do something. "I don't mind."

"I do."

For a moment, Ben hesitated. He didn't want to go against Rider's wishes at such a delicate moment. Ben never obeyed. He headed back to the kitchen without meeting Rider's gaze. Thankfully, the chef hadn't left. Ben didn't know where anything was kept.

He pasted on an apologetic smile. "Jules wants a tray of tea and cookies."

The guy looked rightfully put out. "Sure."

"Sorry. If you show me where everything is, I'll that care of it."

He shook his head. "If it's not a certain way, she won't drink it."

Ben waited, occasionally flashing sympathetic smiles, until the tray was ready. He grabbed it. "Please get out of herc before anyone notices."

With a smile, the staff rushed from the room. Ben headed back to the living room. Rider's eyes flashed with annoyance when he spotted Ben carrying the tray into the room. Ben set it on the coffee table and tried not to meet his stare.

Rider released a tired-sounding sigh. "Go to bed, Ben."

"Benjamin."

Ben cringed at the name.

Thankfully, Rider corrected her. “It’s just Ben. It’s not short for anything.”

Jules blinked. “Well, that’s a bit odd. Ben,” she emphasized his name in a way that set Ben’s teeth on edge. “Pour the tea.”

“He’s not a servant!”

Everyone startled at Rider’s shout. Ben knew this version of Rider. He was about thirty seconds away from saying something he couldn’t take back.

Ben took his hand. “All right. It’s time for everyone to get some rest.”

Even though Ben still felt the rage rolling from Rider, he let Ben lead him from the room. Ben didn’t look back to check anyone’s reactions. He didn’t care about anyone but Rider. As much as he knew Rider wasn’t the only one hurting, Rider was the only one who was his responsibility.

“I’m sorry.”

Ben smiled as he opened Rider’s bedroom door. He knew Rider’s heart. “Don’t apologize. You’re allowed to feel your feelings without shoring up anyone else. He was your dad.”

Rider swallowed. He looked on the verge of tears. Ben didn’t know if he could handle that. Rider was so hard and strong. The idea of him crying was too much. Despite Ben’s ability to deal with anything Rider threw at him, he was very much a crier. If Rider cried, he probably would too. That would embarrass the hell out of him.

“I know I’m your boss.” Rider’s voice broke. He cleared his throat. “I know I’m difficult and I probably make you hate me sometimes. But you're also my best friend and I should've said that before now."

Ben's eyes filled with tears. He blinked rapidly, praying they didn't fall.

"Don't let that go to your head."

An unexpected laugh burst from Ben at that tacked-on tidbit. He sniffed. "I won't, as long as it doesn't go to your head that you're my best friend too."

They shared a small smile.

Rider's fell first. "I don't know how to do this." Rider whispered the confession, as if he couldn't make his voice go any louder. The first tear fell.

Ben didn't think. He hugged him. Rider's arms tightened around him. Ben swiped his eyes on the sly. God, it felt so warm and amazing in Rider's hold. Ben wiped faster as the sad moment brought on all the feels. He was so in love with this man who would never be his. Ben would never get this moment again and it was under the worst of circumstances. His chest hurt for Rider's pain and his own loss. Rider would never love him. Being in his arms drove that point home harder than any other moment between them had.

"Are you crying for me?"

Ben sniffed. "Don't let that go to your head either."

Rider's body shook with laughter.

Ben closed his eyes and dreamed. He breathed Rider's scent into his lungs and memorized the way his body felt. Then he took a step back.

Ben squared his shoulders. “Go to bed. Tomorrow, we’ll take care of everything together.”

For a moment, Rider looked as if he wanted to say something. Instead, he gave Ben a sharp nod. “Good night, Ben. Thank you for coming with me.”

“Of course. That’s what friends are for.” Ben headed for the safety of his assigned room before he did anything stupid. Tomorrow would come soon. They had a funeral to plan.

Chapter Four

Ben was fucking amazing. Rider focused on that to keep himself sane. He was such a force of nature. The entire family fell in line the moment Ben took charge. Rider had never understood how Ben so easily controlled every situation before now. When it wasn't him Ben managed, Rider caught every nuance. He sounded confident—like he knew everything about everything. Then he did that thing with the confidence of a seasoned professional. It was fascinating.

Rider felt certain Ben had never arranged a funeral. At least, not that he had heard. But Ben not only got everything under control, he kept Rider's mom in line. It was masterful. Every time Jules jumped to going overboard, as if his dad would know his casket cost a hundred thousand dollars, Ben reeled her in, keeping her reasonable. There were times Rider nearly laughed at Ben's finesse. His mom tried going crazy on costs. Ben quietly reminded her how many shoes that much could buy. Ben had her number and did it in such a way his mom didn't feel guilty. It was obvious she saw Ben as looking out for her future. And really, he was. With his dad gone, she would likely be bankrupt in under a year. His mom didn't understand moderation. Thankfully, Ben had already talked her down from several ledges and promised to show her how to invest in a way that would keep her in her lavish lifestyle for life.

Listening to the way Ben handled his family made Rider realize how unfair life was to the kindest people. If Ben had Rider's advantages, he could do anything. Instead, he was stuck in a rundown apartment with no car and unable to even buy new clothes. Rider needed to step up. He needed to stop pretending he could live without him. Unfortunately, now wasn't the time to talk about feelings.

The funeral came and went in a blur. Even as his father was laid to rest, nothing felt real. He imagined the shock would fully fade at some point. People milled around his parents' home. They spoke in quiet tones until after the sun fell and the alcohol appeared. Too many people to count had offered their condolences. Rider spotted Ben across the room, sticking to the fringes and looking out of place. Their gazes met. Ben flashed him a reassuring smile. Rider's feet moved his way. Hugh, one of his father's old teammates, stepped in Rider's path before he made it to Ben.

"I don't know if you remember me."

"Of course," Rider said, accepting Hugh's handshake.

Oddly, Hugh didn't release his hand. "I can't tell you how sorry I am for your loss. I work in sports medicine now, specifically with professional athletes. You'd be surprised by the research that's shown a link between sports injuries and cardiovascular events. We're seeing it a lot more these days."

Rider didn't know what to say. He simply nodded.

Hugh patted his hand and still didn't let go. "You're the general manager of the Chuckers now, right?"

"Yes."

"Your dad was really proud of that. He talked about the team all the time."

Rider's throat swelled. He didn't want to have this conversation. Rider wanted to be with Ben. "Dad was proud of all his sons. He always let us know that."

"That's good. He was a good man." Hugh's brown eyes took on a very puppy dog look. "If you need anything, Jules knows how to get in touch with me. I'm always open to working with new teams. So if the Chuckers need anything, let me know."

Ah. There it was. The opportunistic moment. Rider gently tugged his hand away. He needed a stronger drink. "Thank you. I'll keep that in mind. If you'll excuse me."

"Of course." Hugh stepped aside.

Rider's gaze shot to where Ben had been. He was gone. Rider's shoulders fell. He was tired. Rider missed his bed and normal days with Ben. He glanced down at the empty glass in his hand. Surely there was some better whiskey in this house somewhere. Rider would find that first. Then he would hunt down Ben. He needed a real friend.

Ben sat in a lounge by the pool where it was quiet. He couldn't take the discomfort of being surrounded by strangers any longer. It was one thing to be Rider's rock. It was another being subjected to the pompous high society for hours on end. Jules' house was on the beach. The pool overlooked the ocean. A warm breeze ruffled his hair. It was sad this was the closest he had come to a vacation in years. This was the type of place he could never afford.

Matt appeared from nowhere and filled the lounge beside him. "Hey. I see you chose the best seat in the house."

Ben flashed Rider's youngest brother a smile. "It's beautiful here."

Matt nodded. The wind ruffled his dark hair. His eyes were the same light blue as Rider's, but his features weren't as hard. He looked younger and more carefree. "This is a fair turn from my usual scenery."

A soft chuckle fell from Ben's lips. "I imagine so." Matt played for the Canadian pro hockey league. "Halifax, right?"

A huge grin split Matt's face. "I'm surprised you know that."

That caught Ben off guard. "Why? I've worked for your brother for two years."

Matt shrugged. "I just assumed Rider never talks about us. He's never been very..."

Matt made a gesture as if searching for the word.

"Human," Ben supplied.

Matt laughed. "I wasn't going to say that, but sure. Maybe more like he doesn't make friends easily. Most people never see past his prickly personality. To be fair, you've met our mom. She's always leaned too much on Rider. He's forced to draw hard limits with people. I think she taught him all relationships come with strings. If his own mom can't just love him without constant expectations, then surely none of the rest of us can either." Matt stared at the ocean. "At least, that's why I imagine he ran for his life and left us all behind the first moment he could."

It was obvious Matt loved his brother. Ben got it. Rider wasn't always easy to love. “He misses y’all. I can hear it in his voice when he talks about when you were kids. He keeps a file on his computer with all Harlan’s and your stats. It’s kind of funny the way he follows things like he can make you win by obsessing over it.”

Matt chuckled. It was a soft and masculine sound that reminded Ben too much of Rider. “Quiet obsession is Rider’s specialty.”

“I’m aware. That’s why he has ulcers.”

They exchanged a look and burst out laughing.

Matt held his stare for an uncomfortable moment. His smile bled away, but he didn’t break eye contact. “Thank you for everything you’ve done for my family. You haven’t gone unnoticed. My mom." Matt hesitated. Ben waited him out. Matt sighed. "Well, you've met her. I know she loves us. I'm also fairly certain she loved Dad. She loves herself more, though. Always has. This whole nightmare would've been ten times more traumatizing if you hadn't stepped in. We see you."

Ben was more touched by that than he could express. He didn't feel seen often. "It was my pleasure to help how I could." Ben grinned. "I've worked for your brother for two years. My skills at handling difficult people are unmatched."

Matt laughed. "Oh, I'm sure. Rider went through a good thirty assistants before you."

"I'm aware. The entire office warned me not to get comfortable when he hired me." Ben couldn't stop smiling. Matt's upbeat nature was hard to resist.

"Would you like to go for a walk on the beach? This is likely the closest I'll get to a vacation for a while."

Matt's words so closely matched Ben's earlier thoughts. He couldn't resist. "Sure."

Together, they stood and headed for the beach. Matt's company was nice. Ben didn't feel quite as alone as he had since he arrived. Rider had been rightfully tied up in family business. Death was complicated, especially with someone as famous as Rider's father. Despite Ben's involvement in the arrangements, he had been shuffled to the side. That was fine. It was to be expected. Ben still felt out of place and lonely, though.

The walkway narrowed. Their elbows brushed. Matt took his arm and gently steered him down the darkened path. “Be careful. The stones are uneven through here.”

The brush parted. Ben’s breath caught as the ocean breeze hit him full force. The sound of waves had him closing his eyes to savor the moment.

“My brother has always been blind to how lucky he is.”

The softly spoken words had Ben looking Matt’s way.

He watched Ben in a way Ben hadn’t seen from a man in years. It hurt Ben’s chest. Matt looked at him the way Ben always prayed Rider would.

Still, Ben played dumb. Matt was a complication he didn't need. "I don't think that's true. He got those ulcers for a reason. Rider understands exactly how lucky he is to be where he's at. He lives in constant fear of losing it."

A wry smile touched Matt's lips. "I wasn't talking about his career. He has someone completely amazing right under his nose and he doesn't even see it."

Ben looked away. He couldn't risk Matt seeing his heart. "I don't know about that. He pays me really well." Ben wanted to pat himself on the back for his acting skills. If he didn't know himself, he might have thought he truly wasn't more than an employee. A sharp pain sliced through Ben. It was because he wasn't acting. Ben was only an employee. Friend or not, he didn't match Rider. This would never be his life.

Matt touched his elbow. They fell into step next to each other, getting closer to the water before walking along the edge.

"You should send me that file of stats. Maybe it will help me win more."

A laugh burst from Ben. The mood lightened. "I can do that."

"Good. I'll give you my number."

A weight lifted from Ben's chest as Matt fell into a discussion about the Canadian league. Ben found himself drawn into the conversation, fascinated by the difference in rules. He forgot about the reason he was there. The way Rider had ignored him since confessing Ben was his best friend moved to the back of his mind. Ben forgot to hurt over the realization Rider would forever be just out of reach. He decided to just enjoy Matt's company. For a while, Ben let go.

Chapter Five

He heard Ben's laughter before he saw him. The alcohol had his black mood spiraling to something even darker as Ben came into view. He walked elbow to elbow with Matt. They were windblown. They looked happy together. Young. Rider's eye twitched. He fought the urge to lash out. Too much alcohol always made him dumb. That was why he didn't drink often.

Still, Rider lifted his glass to his lips as he watched Ben and Matt's approach. Ben's chin lifted. Rider saw the moment Ben realized he was there. His expression changed. Rider couldn't read him any longer. He exchanged some words with Matt Rider couldn't hear. Matt headed inside while Ben headed his way.

Rider's temper frayed with every step Ben took in his direction. "I'm not paying you to flirt with my brother."

Ben didn't flinch. "I didn't realize you were paying me at all."

That caught Rider off guard. "Of course I am. You work for me."

Ben nodded. "Okay. I'll remember that from now on. Not here as your supportive friend. Noted. Can I get you anything?"

Rider ground his back teeth. He was always one step forward and ten steps back with Ben. Rider was angry with himself, hurting, and pissed at Matt for making Ben laugh when he couldn't. Matt was younger and more personable. He possessed a charm Rider never would. Rider wanted to hurt someone because he hurt. "You're off the clock. Go back to Matt. He likely needs the comfort." Rider walked away, heading down a side path that led to the French doors of his bedroom.

Ben stayed hot on his heels. "No. Obviously, I came here to get as many overtime hours as I could. Tell me what I can do now, or was that your order? Am I being commanded to comfort your brother? He does seem to like me more than you do."

Rider's temper snapped. He chucked the glass he carried without bothering to see where it landed. One second, he was inches from making it inside the safety of his room. The next, Rider had Ben against the wall. Ben stared up at him with defiant eyes, daring Rider to hurt him. The fingers Rider had wrapped around Ben's neck didn't do what Rider expected. He stroked Ben's skin, savoring the moment. His hand moved upward until he held Ben's jaw, keeping him from looking away. Heat built between them, searing Rider's soul.

"You're so fucking blind." The whispered words came from the deep recesses of Rider's heart. He couldn't do this anymore. The dam broke inside him. He touched his lips to Ben's, expecting anything except what happened. Ben grabbed his hair and deepened their kiss—like he had waited a lifetime to taste Rider. A moan escaped him without warning. He had never been so instantly set ablaze. Until he squeezed, Rider didn't realize his hands had moved to Ben's ass, and he had grabbed two handfuls. He didn't stop. Everything about the moment was twice as amazing as he imagined.

"Please?" Even Rider didn't know what he begged Ben to do. Love him. Set him free from his pain. Fix him. Ben was the one who kept him glued together. He needed Ben to read his mind and make it better.

Ben's hands went for the zipper of Rider's pants. A whimper escaped Rider. He was so hard, and he knew it was Ben touching him. Rider couldn't think or function.

Ben's hand dove inside his pants and set his erection free. Rider gasped when Ben squeezed him. His dick throbbed. Ben dropped to his knees on the cobblestone path, and Rider's knees nearly buckled. The way Ben's hot mouth suckled him made Rider whimper. Rider braced one hand on the wall and held Ben's hair with the other. He fucked Ben's mouth. Everything disappeared except the hot suction and the pleasure. Noises came from him he couldn't stop. His hips rolled, taking what he wanted. The maddening pressure built, keeping him thrusting. He didn't think about anything except reaching the edge. Rider held his breath. His muscles tensed. Ben took him to the back of his throat. A loud grunt escaped him as he blew. His hips kept pivoting as Ben sucked him dry. With each passing moment, his skin cooled and his mind cleared. Rider suddenly felt extremely sober. Ben was on his knees in what had to be a painful place. Rocks likely dug into his skin. Yet he kept licking and nuzzling Rider until Rider went soft.

Rider's mind raced at a million miles a minute. That had just happened. There was no taking it back. He couldn't leave Ben unsatisfied. Did Ben even want to be touched? Had this just been a matter of Ben being coerced into thinking Rider expected this of him to keep his job? His breathing hitched. Panic got deeper by the second. There was no air. Was he that guy? Had he become his parents, using employees like personal sex slaves?

Ben was on his feet in a second. He held Rider's face between his hands. "Breathe.

It's okay. I've got you. Just take a breath. I'm here."

Rider followed Ben's lead, breathing in and out. "I didn't..." Rider lost his breath again. He swore everything darkened around the edges. "I would've never..."

Ben kissed him. It was sweet and life-giving. Rider chased his mouth. He forgot to panic. All Rider needed was Ben's lips to survive. In seconds, Rider could breathe again. He had to know. Rider's hand moved south. He cupped Ben through his pants, shaping the erection that was for him. Relief poured through him. Ben wanted him too. Rider could make things even. Ben didn't have to feel exploited.

Rider slid Ben's zipper down as their tongues played. The taste of his cum turned him on more than he cared to admit. He nearly purred the second he held Ben's cock. For such a small guy, he was seriously packing. Rider couldn't stop stroking his length, enjoying the weight of Ben in his hand. He was thick and long. Rider squeezed, fantasizing about what he could do with so much real estate. Rider needed to know more.

He two-handed Ben, exploring his balls too. Damn. He was delicious. Ben moaned. The sound vibrated through their kiss. Rider worked even harder to make Ben come. He needed more of those noises. Rider stroked and squeezed. He pumped faster as Ben's kiss turned frantic. Ben held Rider's shirt in a death grip. Rider turned his head and sucked air, as if he would be the one who blew any second. Ben's mouth moved to his neck. He licked, sucked, and bit.

Rider couldn't be quiet. "Fuck. Give it to me, Ben. Let me finally hear the way you sound as you come. I need to know if my fantasies hold up to the real thing. Let me watch."

A tiny cry, muffled against his skin, broke through the night. Ben's cock jerked in his hand. Cum ran down his fingers. Happiness soared through Rider. That was what he needed. That was what he had been missing. Rider wanted more.

"Come to bed with me."

He didn't want the moment to end. Ben meant everything to him. Rider had to have more.

Ben couldn't say what happened. One second, he gave Rider the argument he obviously wanted. The next, Ben was nude beneath Rider in his bed. His senses were alive. He felt every place they touched. Rider's body was perfection, and it felt damn good against Ben's skin. Their fingers linked as their tongues brushed. Ben refused to think about the consequences. Whatever happened would happen soon enough. For now, he lived his dream.

Rider's mouth moved to his cheek. He kissed a path to Ben's ear. "I'm sorry about earlier. I don't know why I say some of the things I say."

“You’re a porcupine.”

Rider rolled to the side, keeping one leg pinning Ben to bed—like he expected Ben to run. He went up on one elbow and held Ben’s stare. “What?” Ben heard the laughter in his voice.

Ben couldn’t stop trying to keep him happy. “You’re a porcupine. You know, you’re all cute and people want to pet you. But you’re also prickly, which keeps people away, but you were born that way. So.” Ben shrugged.

Rider’s eyes shone bright with happiness. “You just made that up.”

“So what if I did?” Ben couldn’t hide the laughter in his voice. He had never been happier.

Rider kissed his shoulder. Ben felt the way Rider smiled against his skin. “I’m sending you home tomorrow.” It was like getting punched in the gut. Rider kept talking like Ben could still breathe. “You’ve been here too long without a break, dealing with my family. I still have a few days’ worth of loose ends to wrap up here. You probably have a pile of work a mile high on your desk. No one at that arena knows how to survive without you.”

Ben swallowed. “Okay.”

Rider’s expression shifted. Ben obviously wasn’t hiding his thoughts as well as he hoped. “I’m not sending you away. I regret nothing. You don’t deserve the wringer my family has sent you through. I shouldn’t have depended on you so hard these last few days. You deserve better than you get from me ninety percent of the time."

Ben wanted to believe. The timing just felt odd. Still, Ben had never dreamed he would have even this much from Rider. If Rider wanted to breathe and forget this happened, that was what Ben would do. No matter how much it wrecked him. "Just ninety?" Fuck, his throat hurt.

Rider's smile was everything. "Okay. Maybe ninety-five percent. But that five percent I give is golden."

Goddamn. It really was. "Agreed."

Rider's gaze moved over Ben's face. The air changed. Rider stroked Ben's stomach. Ben couldn't look away as Rider lowered his head. When their lips met, Ben's breath caught. He wouldn't regret him. Ben made the vow, praying he could keep it. He didn't want to taint a single second of this memory. Rider was a fleeting dream come true.

Chapter Six

Without Ben to manage his mother, an extra two days became a week. Time got away from him. By the time he made it back to New Orleans, he was completely exhausted. He fell face down across his bed and died for fifteen hours. When his eyes finally opened again, they felt hot. He couldn't hold them open. When the first bout of puking hit, he barely made it to the bathroom in time. He didn't own a thermometer, but he knew he had a fever. The chills made his teeth chatter.

Rider's head pounded so badly, he could barely focus on his phone from the brightness. He had missed a text from Ben.

Ben: *I saw your plane arrived yesterday. Since you're still not back in office, I'll assume you need a few more days. I've informed Tanner and berated him into submission when he insisted three weeks was plenty of time to "suck it up." If you're avoiding me, please just say that so we can move past it and we're not both out of the job.*

Rider had no idea what any of those words meant. He was too dizzy. Still, he managed a quick one-word response.

Rider: *Dying.*

With the phone still clutched to his chest, Rider passed out again. The next time he came to, a cold washcloth covered his eyes. His teeth chattered again. The cool cloth was both a relief and torture. He was so hot yet freezing. Everything hurt—like he felt every painful inch of his skin. His stomach churned. It made loud noises that sounded throughout the quiet room.

"Oh, dear. Put this on your tongue."

Rider heard Ben's voice and obeyed without question. He felt better just knowing Ben was there. For a moment, he wondered if he'd hallucinated until he opened his mouth and a pill dissolved on his tongue. Thankfully, it didn't taste terrible. It was a little fruity with an aspirin aftertaste.

"That'll help with the nausea. When your stomach settles and you think you can keep it down, Dr. Night prescribed you an antiviral medication. It should lessen the symptoms and length."

"Thank you." Rider's voice sounded like shit. He couldn't open his eyes. Not that it mattered, since a washcloth still covered them. His mind cleared a hair. "Wait. I don't want you to get sick."

Ben stroked his stomach like a loving parent would a sick child. "Don't worry about me. Dr. Night started me on meds too, so I wouldn't catch anything."

Rider's muscles relaxed. "Good." A content sigh washed over him as his stomach eased, as if Ben's touch was magic. "That feels good."

"I've got you."

"You always do." Even to Rider's ears, he sounded half asleep already. Darkness tugged at his brain, trying to pull him back into a blissful sleep where sickness couldn't reach him. "That's why I love you."

"I love you too."

Rider heard the smile in Ben's voice, and he knew everything would be okay. Ben would fix him.

Ben stared at Rider's still form and tried to breathe. He wouldn't read too much into their exchange. Rider had said Ben was his best friend. It was entirely possible Rider only meant he loved Ben as he would his best friend. Other types of love existed. Ben couldn't let himself believe Rider meant anything more.

He looked terrible. Ben had been so upset when he had learned Rider was home, but hadn't called or shown up for work. He should have known something was wrong, but their sexual encounter had clouded things. He second-guessed everything now. While Rider hadn't stopped texting him since Ben left Mexico, it had all been business-related. Ben had no idea how to navigate these new waters. He had to stop thinking about it day and night.

Ben checked Rider's temperature one more time. It was still high, but there was nothing he could do about it with Rider asleep. Ben rubbed some hand sanitizer on his hands. He didn't take off his face mask until he left Rider alone to rest. Ben moved through Rider's home as if he had been there a million times, because he had. He ran basically every aspect of Rider's life. Rider's three thousand-square-foot home was nice by most people's standards, but oddly small considering his net worth. Ben knew that number too, since—again—he ran everything. He doubted Rider even knew the code to his safe, much less the numbers to his bank accounts. Ben didn't mind. He enjoyed being Rider's rock. With Rider in his life, Ben didn't have time to focus on himself. That was a good thing. Nothing good waited for him down that road.

He eyed Rider's office as he moved to sit behind the desk. Like his office at the arena, there was nothing personal about it. It was just a home office with office things. Rider's entire house was the same. There were empty rooms. Rooms with furniture that were never used. Thanks to a cleaning service, the place was spotless... and cold. There was no home in his house. Rider lived here and nothing else. Sometimes, it felt like Rider didn't live anywhere. He existed. The team ate his time and attention. Tanner ensured Rider couldn't focus on anything else. Ben wondered if Rider was happy at all, or if he had even stopped long enough to ask himself that.

Ben woke Rider's computer and logged on to their shared workspace. He still had a gazillion emails to answer, new stats he needed to file, and bills to pay. There was a list a mile long of phone calls he needed to return. Dry cleaning pick up and drop off had to be scheduled along with rescheduling all Rider's meetings that had already been rescheduled several times lately. He got to work. His eyes barely left the screen. Time passed with no meaning until the room darkened, making Ben realize he had never turned on the light. The morning sun was so bright in this room, he hadn't even considered it until it began to set. Ben straightened. His back popped. A pain bloomed behind one eye. He squeezed his eyes closed and leaned back in the chair. The pain worsened. Fucking migraines. He hadn't had one in a long time. Ben stood, and the room spun. He gripped the edge of the desk to steady himself. It didn't help. He tried to remember the last time he had eaten. Likely, he was just dehydrated. Sometimes, he got carried away and lost track of drinking and eating. He would raid Rider's fridge. He took a step and then there was nothing.

Chapter Seven

Rider's knee bobbed as he went through Ben's phone. No one had been more surprised than him when the device unlocked with his face. Then he recalled buying the device for Ben and setting it up so he could always reach him. When Ben had started working for him, he had some ridiculous pay-as-you-go phone that failed him more often than not. Rider couldn't have that.

As hard as he tried, Rider couldn't find an emergency contact listed. There was no one programmed as Mom or Dad. Rider racked his brain. He couldn't recall hearing anything about Ben's parents, so he didn't know their names. There were no texts to or from anyone other than him, except Matt, which was a whole other can of worms, and Tanner. Rider wasn't ready to deal with that when he was so fucking scared. He was so sick he couldn't breathe. He wore a face mask, praying no one took his temperature and kicked him out of Ben's hospital room.

A loud crash had torn him from a fever-induced coma. With a spinning head, he had made his way to his office to find Ben on the floor. Blood gushed from a gash where he had hit his head going down. He wouldn't wake, and Rider had never been this goddamn terrified. So he did what he could do; he searched Ben's phone fruitlessly. His gaze kept sliding to the bed. All the machines said Ben was okay. He wasn't reassured. Ben still hadn't opened his eyes even with an ambulance ride and doctor examinations. They had taken blood and stitched his head. Still, he slept. The nurse had tried reassuring him several times. Rider couldn't be comforted right now.

Ben's phone rang, startling him. Rider checked the face. It was Tanner. The sight of the team owner's name reminded Rider he hadn't let anyone know they couldn't work right now. Rider stood and answered as he headed for the door. If he didn't deal with this, Tanner wouldn't stop calling.

"Hello?"

A silent pause met his greeting before Tanner finally spoke. "Rider?"

Rider headed down the hall and stepped outside. "Yes."

"Why are you answering Ben's phone? Never mind. Why aren't you in the office? I've received several calls about your continued absence and now Ben isn't in the office either."

"An emergency has occurred and—"

"I don't want to hear it," Tanner snapped, interrupting him. "You've been flitting around the globe for weeks with one excuse after another. We're inches away from winning the cup and you're fucking around." Rider's temper grew with each word. He was scared shitless about Ben, sick, and he had just lost his father. Something inside Rider snapped.

"For your goddamn information, we're not in the office because Ben is in the hospital. You know good and damn well I do an amazing job running the team despite your constant interference. It's your team and I realize you should get to do what you want, but if you can't handle a few emergencies, then get your ass down here and run it yourself." The more Rider talked, the angrier he got, and the more the resentment showed itself. "Ben and I have worked ourselves into the fucking ground for you for zero appreciation, so you know what? Fuck you. Consider this my resignation. Good luck figuring everything the fuck out." Rider disconnected the call and stormed back inside. Heads turned as he passed. Rider knew fury rolled from him in waves. He couldn't worry about any of that now. Rider had too much happening at once.

When he stepped back inside the room, he found Dr. Night waiting. The dark-haired doctor looked his way while still listening to Ben's chest with a stethoscope. He straightened. "I wondered where you'd gone."

Rider tried calling his temper under control. "There was a call I had to take. Thank you for dropping everything for this. I'm not getting any answers from the ER doctors."

Craig nodded. "They're overrun here. The great flu and Covid collide. You gotta love this time of year." He motioned toward a nearby open laptop. "I just received Ben's medical records. As much as I hate opening myself up to a malpractice suit, this is likely my fault. When Ben called me about you, I didn't think twice about prescribing an antiviral to protect him from catching anything while caring for you. Unfortunately, I'm not his primary doctor, so I didn't have access to his medical records then. Generally, the medication I prescribed is safe for most everyone, but with Ben's immunotherapy treatment, he shouldn't be on that particular antiviral."

Craig's words only confused Rider more. "Immunotherapy?"

Craig nodded. He picked up his laptop and clicked around. Craig spoke with his gaze locked on the screen. "It seems nine months ago he had a cancerous tumor removed from his pancreas. While it appears they feel confident they were able to remove all the cancerous cells, immunotherapy was still recommended since the cancer was apparently more extensive than they believed prior to surgery."

Rider's head spun. Ben had been working for him nine months ago. Surely he would know if Ben had cancer and gotten a tumor removed. A vague memory surfaced. Ben had taken a week's vacation. That week had been hell. When Ben had come back to work, he had moved slower than usual. They had bickered for weeks afterward due to Ben's inability to keep up with him. He'd had a fucking tumor removed and came back to work like nothing happened after less than a week? What the actual fuck? Rider had to shake that off for now.

"Why isn't he waking up?"

“My guess is dehydration combined with low blood pressure and head trauma. Exhaustion. His vitals are perfect now, though. He isn’t comatose. Just sleeping. He’ll be fine. The fluids they’re giving him will help with the dehydration and also to flush the antiviral faster. I’ve looked at his bloodwork. He’s good, Rider. Just relax. Don’t forget you’re sick too.”

Rider nodded, but he felt anything but reassured. While Ben looked like he slept peacefully, Rider wanted to see his beautiful hazel eyes.

“I’ll come by the house and check on him again in the morning. Once he’s awake and moving, he’ll be released. They don’t have beds available to admit him over this.”

Rider kept bobbing his head, agreeing to everything. He had no idea why. Not an ounce of information sank into his brain. All he thought about was that tumor. Then he was alone with Ben and didn't recall saying his goodbyes. His gaze dropped to Ben's phone again. Not only had he not known about Ben's struggles, he didn't know who to call. He was so fucking angry, confused, and frustrated with himself. Rider had let his career cloud everything. He had taken and taken from Ben while Ben listened and gave him everything. Ben had shown up and stayed through every horrible life event in the past two years, and Rider didn't even know who to fucking call.

He unlocked Ben's phone again. Rider's lawyer's number was listed in his contacts. Rider hit the call icon. Richard answered on the second ring, proving how much respect Ben commanded. Rider's calls were never answered so fast.

"Hello?"

"Hey, Rich. It's Rider."

"Mr. Bailey. How are you?"

Rider ignored the question. "I need you to do something morally questionable for me."

"That's what you pay me to do."

Good. He had been prepared to bribe him. "I need you to do a thorough investigation on Ben."

A pregnant pause met his request. Richard cleared his throat. "Um. Okay. How thorough?"

Rider didn't hesitate. "I want to know everything, including a copy of health records."

"All right. I know a guy. It likely won't take long."

"Good." A thought hit. "Send the file to my phone."

"Okay. Is everything okay?"

Rider wanted to say no. He wanted to tell everyone he was a piece of shit. "Yeah. It's not for a bad reason. There's just something I'm trying to find."

"Oh. Okay." Richard sounded relieved. "Give me an hour or so. I'll have your file."

"Thanks, Richard. I appreciate it."

"No problem."

Rider disconnected the call and went back to staring at Ben. It was time to focus on him now. Rider had been selfish long enough.

A throbbing pain woke Ben. "Ow." He reached up to rub his forehead. His fingers met some type of sticky tape. He pried his heavy eyelids open. Rider slept in a chair next to him, wearing a face mask. His skin was blood red. Ben looked around. He was in a hospital room, but it wasn't a typical room. It looked like the ER. Ben sifted through his thoughts. He had been working in Rider's office. That was it. He didn't remember anything after that.

"Rider."

He didn't budge.

Ben tried again, a little louder. "Rider."

Rider shot upright like he had been prodded with a sharp stick. He blinked at his surroundings, as if just as confused as Ben.

"You should be in bed."

Rider's gaze swung his way. "Hey. You're awake. How are you feeling?"

"Confused." Ben's voice sounded groggy. He couldn't control it.

"What do you remember?"

"Working in your office."

Rider nodded. "You lost consciousness and hit your head. I couldn't get you to wake, and you were bleeding pretty heavily. It's a good thing I called an ambulance, though. Otherwise, the meds Dr. Night prescribed you might've killed you."

Ben blinked. His head cleared a little more by the second. "Really? Whoa. Who knew an antiviral could kill anyone?"

"Definitely not me, since you never tell me anything."

Ben's head pounded. He had no idea what Rider meant. "I talk to you every day."

"Then why didn't you tell me you had a tumor removed?"

Ben barely stopped himself from rolling his eyes. “They got all the cancer cells. It was no big deal.”

Rider’s eye twitched the way it always did when he was suppressing his anger. “I’m sick right now. We both need to get some rest. Just know we’re talking about this when I’m well.”

“Talking about what?”

“You don’t have to always take care of everything alone,” Rider said, finally exploding.

Ben made a dismissive gesture. “I’ve been taking care of everything alone my entire life. It’s no big deal.”

Rider’s gaze turned pleading, making Ben realize this was way more important to him than Ben realized. “But you’re not alone. You have me. I want to know what's going on in your life."

Someone knocked on the door. Lauren stuck her head inside the room. "Hey."

Lauren had worked in Chuckers' media relations for years before Ben had been hired. They spoke a lot, but he had no idea why she was here.

"Hey. Come in."

She stepped fully into the room, holding a huge and expensive-looking vase of flowers. Lauren set them on the first flat surface she spotted. "These are from Mr. Paige. He also wanted me to tell you to take however much time you need. Your job will still be waiting for you." Her gaze moved Rider's way. "That goes for you too."

Ben met Rider's stare. "Oh, dear. What did you do? Tanner is never nice unless you're mean to him. I'm pretty sure it's his kink."

Lauren laughed. It was an uncomfortable sound. "Well, I have to get to the office. Despite this errand, you know Mr. Paige still expects me to show up on time."

That didn't surprise Ben. "Thank you. I'm sure I'll bc back by tomorrow."

Rider growled.

Ben released a quiet sigh. It seemed they wouldn't be getting along for a while. A blowjob had changed nothing. There was some comfort in that.

"See you later." Lauren waved over her shoulder as she left.

Ben's gaze returned to Rider. "What did you do?"

"I heard you were awake. Are you ready to go home?"

Ben took a calming breath at yet another interruption. He smiled at the nurse. "Yes. Thank you."

She nodded. "You need to follow up with Dr. Night. Is this your ride home?" She pointed toward Rider.

Rider nodded. "I'll get us home."

The blonde smiled. "Good. He also can't be alone for the next twenty-four hours. Will you be with him?"

"He won't be alone." Rider's reassurance sounded like it came from the heart. Ben didn't know what to think.

She went to work unhooking the IV and heart monitor. "I'll get the paperwork started. It should move pretty quickly since we're short rooms right now."

"I appreciate it." Ben really wanted to take something for his headache and go back to sleep. Plus, Rider looked like he felt like shit.

The moment they were alone again, Ben's gaze shot Rider's way. Even with a mask hiding half his face, Ben could tell he tried playing innocent.

"What?"

"Tanner. Spill."

Rider shrugged. "I might've told him to bring his lazy ass down here and run the team."

Ben's eyebrows rose. "And?"

"I resigned."

Ben took a steadying breath. "Well, it seems he didn't accept." Thank God, since Rider's resignation put him out of the job.

"That doesn't mean I accept his non acceptance."

Ben did not feel well enough to deal with this. Rider always picked the moments Ben was at his lowest to be the most difficult.

"Let's just go get some sleep." What Ben really needed was a drink... and for Rider to stop looking at him like he might drop dead any second.

Chapter Eight

WITH BEN TUCKED IN beside him, acetaminophen running through his veins, and a broken fever, Rider felt a lot better. Ben slept peacefully, as if he hadn't already slept through the night at the ER. Rider felt oddly awake for someone who dozed off and on all night. He couldn't stop thinking about the report Richard had sent or how casually Ben admitted to handling everything alone. A background check had been run on Ben when they hired him, but juvenile records were sealed. Rider couldn't have known Ben had been kicked out by his parents at fourteen. He had lived on the streets, in and out of jail until he turned seventeen. Then a charity that helped gay teens rejected by their parents to find shelter and education for a successful future had stepped in. Ben really had handled everything alone. He wasn't alone now. Rider saw him.

He ran his fingers through Ben's hair. Ben shivered in his sleep. Rider tucked him in tighter. He was still so fucking angry with himself for not paying attention and a little mad at Ben for always nearly killing himself for Rider's sake. Ben could've died coming back to work that soon after such a major surgery. As much as Rider understood now, Ben was drowning in medical debt, but Ben should have said something. Rider would never let him struggle. But Ben never told him anything. It was like Ben didn't see him as human, and it was Rider's fault.

Since hanging up his skates, Rider had fought so fucking hard to hang on to hockey. It destroyed everything in his life, especially him. He had turned into an unfeeling robot who put work over everything. Then this gorgeous and maddening fireball had burst into his life, refusing to put up with his shit. Rider couldn't live without him. So Ben had to let him in.

Rider kissed his forehead.

"You should be sleeping." Ben sounded more asleep than awake.

"Don't worry. I'll fall asleep soon."

Ben snuggled closer. "Good. I need you better."

"I'll be fine." Because he had Ben. That was all he needed.

Ben stared at the expanse of Rider's shoulders. There was a sexy spot between his shoulder blades that called for Ben's lips. He scooted closer, trying not to wake him. All he had to do was kiss that spot, and he would know if Rider still had a fever. He gave in to temptation. A sexy chuckle made Ben's lips vibrate with them pressed against Rider's back.

"Do you plan to do anything with that?"

"What?"

Rider shifted, pressing his ass against Ben's erection. "That."

Ben hid a smile.

"I can feel you smiling against my skin."

Ben kissed him again because he couldn't resist. "I would never molest a sick man."

"I've never been too sick to get molested in my entire life."

They had stripped to their underwear before going to bed. There was so much sexy muscle on display. Ben couldn't resist him. His lips found that same spot between Rider's shoulders. He dipped his hand inside Rider's underwear at the hip, peeling it down a hair.

"I know you like getting blown. What else do you like?"

Rider took a ragged-sounding breath and Ben knew he was hard for him. "I'm kind of partial to getting fucked, but I'm willing to do whatever it takes to watch you come."

God, he was perfect. They had spent one night touching, but the topic of preferences hadn't been discussed. Rider gave off top energy. Ben would rather not bottom, but—like Rider—he would happily do whatever it took to make Rider blow. He just wanted to be with Rider.

Ben hummed against Rider's skin as he pushed Rider's underwear down another inch. "There's nothing I want more than to be inside you."

Rider whimpered in a way that had Ben leaking pre cum.

Ben urged Rider onto his stomach. He straddled Rider's body and kissed his nape. "You're still on the mend. Just rest. I'll take care of you."

Rider didn't move or makc a sound—like he was afraid Ben would stop if he disobeyed.

Condoms and lube sat on the bedside table. Ben tried not to think about that too much. He grabbed both and moved them to the bed, where he could find them later. First, he wanted to explore and enjoy every inch of Rider. He had spent too many nights dreaming. Ben had to know if reality lived up to fantasy.

He slowly stripped Rider of his underwear as he kissed a path down Rider's spine. Ben stopped to nibble his ass cheek. Damn. The globes of his ass were so firm and perfect. Years of skating showed in his powerful lower body. Once Ben had Rider nude, he quickly stripped off his own underwear so he would be ready the instant he needed to be. His lips found Rider's skin again. He licked the small of Rider's back.

Rider made a sound that had Ben hiding a smile.

Ben opened a condom and rolled it down his length. He wet his fingers with the lube. His lips stayed glued to Rider's back as he shifted positions, urging Rider to make room for him between his thighs. Ben fought the urge to impale him immediately. That wasn't really what he wanted. Ben needed Rider to know he was worshiped. There was no one else out there who wanted Rider as badly as Ben. No one else would put him on a pedestal the way Ben would.

He coated the outside of his condom in lube as he kissed his way lower. Rider breathed harder by the second, openly anticipating Ben's next move. He wouldn't make Rider wait. Ben grabbed Rider's ass cheeks and spread them, going face first between them. His tongue found Rider's asshole. Rider whimpered while Ben licked and prodded. He moved restlessly beneath Ben. Ben tortured him until Rider begged.

"Please?"

It was the quietest of whispers. Ben didn't miss it. He shot upward and pressed his crown against Rider's waiting hole. Ben froze. He waited until he felt Rider's muscles relax. Then he thrust.

The cry that tore from Rider was everything. It was pure need. Ben dug his knees into the mattress and took Rider's ass. He was hot and tight. Greedy. Ben thought he might go insane. He hadn't been inside anyone in almost three years. Plus, Rider was his biggest fantasy. Ben had to keep his back teeth locked to stop himself from coming immediately. He shifted positions until a deep moan vibrated from Rider. At the sound, Ben went to work. He pounded that spot that would drive Rider wild.

Neither of them spoke. It was like they were both too lost in the reality of the moment. Ben had the only man he wanted. He couldn't focus on words. Nothing mattered except ensuring Rider came back for more. Unlike Rider, Ben had nothing else to offer. He didn't have money, fame, or even a family. But Ben would love him and fuck him like no one else ever had before. Rider could leave him behind any time he liked, but he would damn well remember Ben.

Rider's muscles tensed.

Ben held his breath and kept up the pace.

Rider's entire body jerked while he muffled a cry with his face buried in the mattress. His body convulsed, milking Ben. Ben bit his bottom lip and squeezed his eyes closed. His entire being focused on the pressure climbing his cock. Then ecstasy. A loud pant burst from him as his dick jumped and spat inside Rider's ass. Breathy whimpers sounded muted against Rider's skin. His orgasm was top tier. He had wanted to come just like this for much longer than he cared to admit, even to himself. Rider was so much more of everything than anyone else. He was exhilarating and maddening. Rider was Ben's personal rollercoaster. Ben couldn't get enough. He prayed this didn't end.

Truthfully, Rider still felt sick as hell. His muscles ached and his head pounded. But for a while, Ben had taken all that away. Ben had eaten his ass, fucked him senseless, and then cleaned him up and tucked him into bed. Spoiled didn't begin to cover the way Ben treated him. Things should have been the other way around. Ben was the one with a set of stitches and an ambulance ride under his belt. Rider would make them even. He swore it.

For now, his eyelids felt too heavy.

Rider didn't want to fall asleep. Ben was in the shower. He watched the door, waiting to see him again. His gaze moved toward the dresser where they had left the flowers from Tanner. He supposed he should go back to work. Ben needed his job... unless he could convince Ben to let him take care of him. Rider's eyes slid closed. Ben was too independent. He would never want to be that reliant on Rider.

The bed dipped beside him. Rider's eyes shot open. It was dark. He didn't recall falling asleep, but the day was gone. "What time is it?"

"Sorry. I didn't mean to wake you. It's ten p.m."

Rider snagged Ben's waist and hauled him against his chest, tucking him tightly against his body. A content sigh escaped him. "That's better." He slid his hand up Ben's bare stomach to his chest, savoring every second until he reached Ben's heart. Rider closed his eyes and focused on the steady thump against his palm. He had never felt less alone in his life. Rider knew at that moment he would never be happy sleeping without Ben again. "I'll go back to work tomorrow."

"If you're feeling up to it and that's what you want, then that's cool with me."

Rider kissed Ben's ear. "I don't know if it's what I want, but it's the adult thing to do, I suppose. But I also need to set some boundaries with Tanner, and we can't keep killing ourselves for zero appreciation. I want our nights to be like this. Not at the office, scrambling to make deals happen."

"Okay. I'll help you talk to Tanner."

"No." This one time, Rider didn't want that. "You'll try to smooth things over, and I don't want that. I'm tired of getting walked on and micromanaged." He squeezed Ben, hugging him because he couldn't resist. "But I also don't want you to worry. No matter what happens, you won't be unemployed. I'd never knowingly let you struggle. We'll talk more about that tomorrow."

"All right. I trust you."

That was all Rider needed to hear. He planned to take good care of Ben. "Goodnight, baby."

"Goodnight."

Rider heard the smile in Ben's voice. That was good. Rider would keep him that way. First, Tanner. Then, he would build them something new and better. They were done with the constant hustle. It was time to focus on them. Rider planned to take over Ben's life in a whole new way. He couldn't wait to feel better, so he could give Ben the attention he deserved.

Chapter Nine

If Ben claimed he wasn't nervous, he would be lying. Rider had flown to Canada, leaving him behind at the office. Ben swung heavily between staying focused on work and keeping his gaze locked on Rider's location on his phone. He had forced himself to keep his phone put away for two hours now. It was fucking hell.

Ben knew Rider wouldn't let him go unemployed. But Ben didn't have the luxury of not totally worrying about it. Rider was amazing, but he didn't think too much about other people's struggles. He had no clue what it was like to live paycheck to paycheck. Ben wasn't sure what losing his job here meant for him. He couldn't control things if he didn't obsessively consider every angle.

A light knock on the open office door pulled Ben from his thoughts and brought his gaze shooting toward the door. Matt stood in the doorway, looking unsure of his welcome.

He gave Ben a small wave. "Hey."

A bright smile snapped to Ben's lips. "Hey. Come in. What brings you by?"

Matt stepped inside the office. His gaze moved toward Rider's empty desk before settling on Ben again. “I came to see my brother.”

Ben chuckled. “I figured that much. This is just a long way for an unexpected visit. Not that I’m not thrilled to see you.”

Matt’s unsure smile turned genuine. “I’m happy to see you too.” His light blue gaze moved over Ben’s face. “What happened to your head?”

Ben winced. He knew it looked awful. What had been stitches yesterday was now also a large ugly-looking bruise. “I fainted and hit my head. It’s a long story.” He pointed at a chair next to the edge of his desk. “Sit. Tell me why you came all the way from Canada for an unexpected visit.” Ben knew it wasn’t his business. He still planned to be nosey.

Matt sat. The unease returned to his features. "Is Rider here? I hate to make you listen to this story twice."

Uh-oh. "He had a morning meeting with Tanner in Toronto." Ben pulled his phone from his desk. "Let me check his location." Honestly, he was glad for the excuse to check again. A smile he couldn't control snapped to Ben's lips. "He's thirty minutes away from the airport. So it'll be about an hour before he makes it back to the office."

Matt nodded. He rubbed the back of his neck. His gaze moved in every direction except Ben's. "Do you want to get some lunch or something while we wait?"

Ben's unease grew by the second. He couldn't think of any reason for Matt to be this nervous. "Sure. I can order us something, so we don't risk missing Rider's arrival."

"Sounds good." Matt finally met his stare again. "I won't get you in trouble, will I?"

"For what?" The question truly caught Ben off guard.

Matt shrugged. "I don't know. Rider doesn't seem to like it when we hang out."

Ben snorted. "He'll be fine. What aggravates Rider changes daily. You can't tiptoe around any perceived slights with him. What looks like anger over one thing could very well just be him pissed his suits weren't properly pressed."

Matt laughed. Some of the rigidness left his shoulders. "So he hasn't changed much over the years, then."

It always piqued Ben's curiosity when Rider's family spoke as if they hadn't seen him in several years. He knew Rider hadn't spent much time with them in the two years Ben had worked for him. In his defense, hockey had a packed schedule and his brothers both had pro careers just as busy. It made coordinating visits nearly impossible. Still, they were brothers. Ben had so many questions. Instead of asking a single one, they scrolled food apps on Ben's phone and found something to eat. They chatted about nothing while they waited. Ben made it halfway through eating before he circled back around again.

"Do you not have any upcoming games?"

Matt set his burger aside and wiped his fingers on his napkin. He went back to avoiding Ben's gaze. "I was released from the team."

Ben's heart dropped. "Oh no. Why?" It was a dumb question. Ben was the one who gathered Matt's stats for Rider. They weren't good.

Matt shrugged. "I'm not really living up to the same potential in majors that I showed in minors." He met Ben's stare again. "It's a shitty thing to do, I know, since we never speak. I'm really hoping Rider can help me find work, but I doubt he'll appreciate me asking."

"Nonsense. He's your brother, and he has connections. I'm sure he can pull some strings for you." Ben had to be honest. "It likely won't be majors, though. The Chuckers are too close to winning the cup for him to disrupt the team. If they don't go all the way this year, Rider and I will likely be out of the job too."

Matt's relief was palpable. "Minors is fine. Anything is better than nothing. I don't want to go back to living with Mom."

Ben patted his arm. "It'll be okay. You'll see."

"What will be okay?" Rider asked as he strolled into the room.

Matt turned in his chair so fast, it had to have hurt his back. "Rider. Hey. I've been waiting for you."

Rider flashed a kind smile. "I see that. This is a long way to come to have lunch."

Matt looked like he might puke. "Actually, I came to beg for a favor."

Rider took off his suit jacket and draped it on the back of his chair. Ben's gaze followed every move. His mouth watered.

He was so in love and hungry to touch Rider.

"That's unsurprising. What's up?"

Ben's hackles rose a bit at Rider's tone. This was his younger brother, and he needed help. Ben stepped in, ensuring Rider understood he expected Rider to help.

"Your brother needs you to pull some strings for him. He's been released from the Canadian league. You have a ton of connections. Surely the Blue Fires would love to have him."

Rider stared at Matt as if he was the one who spoke. "No."

Rage unexpectedly punched Ben in the chest. Matt was obviously scared for his future and Rider was being so callous.

“Please wait in the hall, Matt. I need to speak to your brother privately.”

Matt didn’t hesitate to run for the hills. Ben didn’t know what he heard in Ben’s voice, but Matt darted into the hall and shut the door behind him.

The moment they were alone, Ben went both feet in. “What the fuck was that? Your brother needs you and you’re just ‘no?’”

“Yes.”

Ben blinked. “Why? Surely if you needed help, and he had the connections, he would help you.”

Rider sat on the edge of his desk. He cocked his head to one side, studying Ben. “Why does this matter so much to you?”

"Because he's family," Ben answered, wondering why that wasn't obvious. "He loves you, admires you, and needs you right now."

Rider didn't budge. "Trust me. If I get him a spot with the Blue Fires, nothing will improve for him."

The way Rider dismissed his brother's plight made Ben feel a way he didn't like. "I don't know if I can love someone who so callously dismisses their baby brother. He came to you for help. He needs you." Ben heard the way his voice cracked. He couldn't help it. Rider's attitude unlocked something in him Ben didn't like. It triggered things he tried to keep buried.

"I didn't say I wouldn't help. Just not that way. If I get him a spot on the team, he'll always know he didn't earn it and he'll play like he doesn't deserve it. Everyone on that team will treat him like he's a pity player. If he wants to play this game, he has to work for it. What I don't understand is why you're this upset by my decision. Do you have feelings for my brother?"

Ben didn't have the energy to yell the way he wanted. Rider's coldness cut him. "No. I want you to feel something for your brother. If you can't or don't, what hope is there for me? I'm no one. You have these people who love you and you act like they don't exist."

Rider slid from the desk and moved to the chair Matt had vacated at the edge of Ben's desk. "You don't understand, baby. This is when I hear from them. When they need something, this is the only time I see or hear from my family."

"You're the one who doesn't understand. At least Matt is here. You don't know what's it like. It's obvious you don't know how much you have. You've never had to stand outside your parents' house and beg them to let you back inside. Plead for them to love you unconditionally the way a parent should. Or hell, just let you have your shoes and jacket, so you don't freeze. You have a family that loves you. Stop shutting your brother out. He still wants you." Ben shrugged, feeling insecure now that the words were out there. Still, he didn't stop. "I've never had that." Even Ben heard how defeated he sounded. "How can I trust that I'll get it from you when you act this cold?"

Rider stood. He headed for the door. Ben focused on his desk and blinked. He didn't want to cry. His eyes burned.

He hated everything about everything he had just said. Ben had exposed himself in a way that left him raw. He had projected, and he knew it. Until that moment, he hadn't realized how insecure he felt about this relationship. His skin felt cold. He had to get out of here.

Matt stared at his shoes as he walked away from the arena. Downtown New Orleans had several bars. He would find one and drown his sorrows. There had been no sense in waiting for Ben to berate Rider. Rider was right. Matt didn't deserve to have Rider pull any strings. He had come here out of pure panic and desperation. Matt had always been the disappointment in the family. The black sheep. Rider was the rock. Harlan was the wild child. Matt was the one who always fucked up. He got it. Matt made Rider tired. That was why he tried staying away. Rider didn't deserve to continually deal with the family's bullshit, and everyone always turned to him. He was the only one of them who wasn't a complete flake. Rider had his shit together. Maybe Matt could go back to school or something. His shoulders fell. He already had an engineering degree, and that was the last fucking thing he wanted to do with his life. What would he do? Get a master's in uselessness? He was so fucking done with everything.

With his head down, Matt nearly plowed some guy down as they crossed paths on the sidewalk. "Oh, shit. Sorry."

The guy didn't even look his way as he climbed into the back of a waiting car. Matt watched. The guy had wide shoulders and dark hair. He was built like a fucking linebacker in an expensive suit. It was obvious even a stranger on the street knew Matt wasn't worth their time.

Matt started to walk away. He noticed a wallet on the ground. Matt scooped it up and flipped it open. It belonged to the guy in the car. Matt ran toward it. "Excuse me. You dropped your wallet."

The car pulled away from the curb. Matt's shoulders fell. He checked the guy's information. William Slater White. He lived in town. Matt pulled out his phone and searched for the listed address. It was a thirty-minute walk. Matt had time. He had nothing but fucking time. Matt's phone rang. Rider's name popped up.

With a sigh, Matt answered. He deserved a lecture. "Hello?"

"Where in the hell did you go? Get back in here so we can discuss your options."

For a moment, Matt stared at nothing while he chewed his bottom lip. All the times Rider had stepped in and swept up his mess ran through Matt's head. He couldn't keep doing this to Rider. Their entire family had already turned Rider cold. Matt didn't want to be part of that anymore. "Nah. I'm good. You're right. I don't deserve to ask you for help. You can do me another favor, though." Matt didn't give Rider time to speak. "Love Ben the way he deserves. He's so fucking in love with you. I can hear it when he talks about you, and he lights up every time you walk in the room. You're an idiot if you don't give him the world. Plus, you deserve to be the kind of happy he would make you. Love you. Have a good life." Matt disconnected the call and went back to staring at the directions to his stranger's house. He had a long walk ahead of him and nothing but time.

Ben wouldn't look at him. He threw Matt's and his lunch away with his head down and gaze averted. The darkness vibrating from him made Rider feel a little sick. He had never been good at expressing his feelings. Rider came from a family dynamic Ben didn't understand. Ben was right. They loved Rider. But they had always loved what Rider could do for them more than they loved him.

Before today, Rider thought he wanted Ben to open up to him about his past. Now that he had caught a glimpse of the pain Ben kept hidden, Rider just wanted to make the past disappear.

"I tried."

Ben didn't look his way. "I know."

Rider couldn't do nothing. "Look, Ben. I know you want to believe I have a good family."

“No,” Ben said, cutting him off. “I should’ve stayed out of it. Your family has nothing to do with me. How did the meeting go with Tanner?”

Damn. Rider knew that tone. Ben had put him firmly back into the role of being his boss. “I told him this was my final season with the team.”

Ben’s head shot up. Rider nearly took a step back at what he saw in Ben’s eyes. He was angry, broken, and maybe even hated Rider a little. Rider couldn’t breathe. Before he could explain, Ben went back to cleaning his desk. “It’s your decision, of course. I still have three weeks of personal time accumulated. Since there’s only two weeks left before the cup is awarded, I’ll use what I have left to finish out the season.”

It hit Rider. Ben was cleaning his desk. He was clearing it out. “What are you doing?”

Ben didn’t stop. “Hopefully, the team will go all the way and make it easier for me to find a new job.”

“Seriously, Ben. What in the fuck are you doing?”

“Please forgive my recent indiscretions. I’d appreciate it if you wouldn’t mention that if anyone calls for a reference. I can’t afford to be out of work.”

Desperation clawed at Rider. He couldn’t lose Ben. “For fuck’s sake, Ben. Just stop. I would never kick you to the curb and leave you homeless the way your parents did. My love is real.”

Ben's hard gaze met his. Rider realized his mistake too late. "How do you know that about my parents?"

Rider's gaze slid away. "You just told me while arguing Matt's case."

"No. How do you know that?"

Rider blew out a breath. "I had you investigated."

"When?"

Rider held Ben's stare. "When I found out about the cancer and realized how much you've been keeping from me." Rider stood. His anger brought him to his feet without him noticing. Ben wasn't the only one who had a reason to be pissed. He leaned on the desk, going nearly nose to nose with Ben. "For two years, I've let you all the way in. We've spent countless hours talking about my neurotic mom, my playboy brother who probably has at least three kids he doesn't acknowledge, and my other brother who can't seem to function as an adult. You've been privy to my every thought while you keep me at arm's length." Rider tapped his chest. "I'm the one who gets treated like I'm not human, and maybe I am colder than most people, but there's no damn way you don't know I love you. There's nothing I wouldn't give for you. Hell, I quit this job because Tanner said I had to choose, because—according to him—my relationship with you is just a lawsuit waiting to happen. There's nothing or no one who could tear me away from you. You're the one who can't say the same. You're the one not letting me in. Maybe I'm not the one who's cold."

A tear slipped down Ben's cheek, ripping out Rider's heart. "Please don't quit because of me. You love this team."

Rider's anger disappeared at the quiet pain in Ben's voice. "I love you more." Rider moved to Ben's side. He sat on the edge of the desk and pulled Ben to stand between his knees. Rider held Ben so he couldn't get away. "There's so much more I want from life than working myself into the ground so Tanner's team can be the best. I want to marry you and take you to see the world. Baby, I'm tired. I just want to be with you."

More tears fell. Ben sniffed. He looked so beautiful with his red nose. Rider's heart had never stood a chance. The phone on Ben's desk rang. Without looking away from Rider, he pressed the speakerphone button. "Rider Bailey's office."

"Hey, Ben. This is Tanner. I have a plane waiting to bring you to Canada. We need to discuss your future now that Rider is leaving us. On your way, think about what you'll need to move here and work for me personally."

"Get fucked, Tanner." Ben disconnected the call. His arms wound around Rider's neck as he shuffled closer. "Well, I just ensured I'll never work in this field again."

Despite how terrible the day had been so far, Rider couldn't stop smiling. He knew Ben. Ben wouldn't leave him. "That's okay. Working would get in the way of us traveling."

"I never said yes."

"You will."

Ben shook his head. “I can’t even imagine what it must be like to be as cocky as you.”

Rider swiped the tears from Ben’s cheeks. “It’s not cockiness. I love you. I love you so fucking much that it’s impossible for you not to know we belong together. When I got to Tanner’s, and he started his usual bullshit, it hit me. It’s not this job that I’ve fought so hard to keep to the point of giving myself ulcers. I want to stay with you. I knew if I lost this job, then I’d lose you.”

Ben shook his head. His shoulders lifted in a small shrug. “I’m not sure it’s possible for you to lose me. Not really.” He took an unsteady-sounding breath. “I’m sorry I projected my past onto you. For the most part, your family is horrible.”

A bark of unexpected laughter burst from Rider.

Ben didn't stop. "However, I do honestly believe Matt wants a real relationship with you. In Mexico, he had a lot of pride in his voice when he talked about you. Everything aside, though, you're right. I am cold."

"I shouldn't have said that—"

Ben covered Rider's mouth, cutting off his words. "No. You're right. I'm terrified of being shut out by the person I love the most. It's already happened once in my life. There has been a small part of me I kept locked away from you. I love you. More than anything. That gives you the power to completely destroy me." Ben took a ragged-sounding breath. "But I know you won't."

Rider kissed Ben's fingers, reminding him he still had Rider's mouth covered.

Ben dropped his hand.

"Marry me."

Ben took another shaky-sounding breath at Rider's words. "Okay."

Rider touched his forehead to Ben's. Up close, his hazel eyes looked more yellow than green. Beautiful. "I still feel like shit, baby."

Ben chuckled. "You shouldn't have come back to work yet. No fever doesn't equal not sick."

Rider nodded. "Let's go home." He kissed Ben's forehead and slipped from the desk. It had been a hectic day. He had experienced every possible emotion before noon. Now he just wanted to get better so he could marry Ben. Nothing else mattered anymore.

Chapter Ten

"You'd look amazing in this. We're getting it."

Ben eyed the seafoam-colored Polo shirt Rider held and hung on to his temper by a thread. "Oh my God. Stop. You don't have to buy everything you see."

Rider flashed him an evil smile. "Married two weeks and already our first fight about money."

Ben covered his eyes. “There’s no fight. It’s your money. You can buy whatever you want. I just—”

Rider covered his mouth. “Nope. Say less. You’re upset I’m spending too much of our money.”

Ben bit him.

Rider roared with laughter and ran for the closest register. He was like a giant kid. All Ben could do was shake his head and smile in spite of himself. Retirement looked damn good on Rider. It had been three months since the Chuckers had won the cup. The phone calls hadn’t stopped coming from people wanting to lure Rider to manage their team. Rider hadn’t shown an ounce of interest in doing anything except being Ben’s husband. He looked so much happier. His ulcers had healed. He definitely acted twenty years younger.

Ben slapped Rider's ass as he reached the checkout lane where Rider waited.

Rider motioned over his shoulder. "See how abused I am?"

The cashier smiled. It was obvious she just wanted to do her job and move on with her life. Ben glanced around, making sure no one watched. He pressed against Rider's back and kissed him between the shoulder blades. With the tall counter hiding his actions, Ben quickly stole a feel of Rider's junk.

Rider looked over his shoulder, tossing Ben a laughing glance.

Ben flashed an innocent smile. "What?"

"You'll pay for that one."

Ben couldn't wait. He knew he had thrown fire on Rider's playful side. He adored this new Rider. This version of Rider was less maddening in an angering way, and more the might embarrass him at any time maddening.

"I mean, I have to reimburse you for the shirt." Ben batted his eyelashes at him.

A low growl vibrated from Rider. He grabbed his new purchase and Ben's hand. Ben smiled like an idiot as Rider practically dragged him to the parking lot. Driving Rider insane never got old. The moment they were inside their car with the air running, Rider was across the console. He massaged Ben's cock through his shorts while his tongue filled Ben's mouth. Ben's hips lifted, seeking more of the rough touch. Rider always set him ablaze faster than expected.

A ringing filled the car.

Rider groaned against Ben's lips. "We never get any fucking peace. Let's skip the country and change our names."

Ben laughed. "I just changed my name."

With an exasperated sigh, Rider moved back to the driver's seat. They both groaned when they spotted Tanner's name on the screen of the dashboard.

"Go ahead and answer it. He won't stop calling until you do."

Rider didn't look happy about it, but he did as told. He tapped the screen, accepting the call. "This is Rider."

"It's Tanner. I have one final offer for Ben and you. There's a plane waiting."

Rider rubbed his forehead. “Ben and I have told you several times we’re not interested. We’ve only been back from our honeymoon one day and we’re ready for a quiet life.”

“Nonsense. You two will be bored and killing each other in under two months. You’re too smart and driven to do nothing for the rest of your lives.”

A sexy smirk touched Rider’s lips. “I wouldn’t say we’re doing nothing.”

A loud huff came through the line. “Please, at least meet with me. The limited contract Medvedkov signed is up and Coach Murphy and he are already being courted by Phoenix again.”

Even though Ben was the only person looking at him, Rider shrugged. “So, pay them what they’re worth.”

"I've already agreed to do that, but they're both still making noises like they'll walk unless I bring you both back onboard. It seems Medvedkov has had some run-ins in the past with your possible replacement. He's not interested in being trapped in a contract that leaves him managed by someone he hates."

Ben and Rider exchanged a look. No matter what, they had the Chuckers in their blood.

"Hold on a second." Rider muted the call. "What do you want to do here? We have to make this decision together."

Ben chewed his bottom lip. He didn't want to lose this new playful Rider, but he also knew Rider would blame himself if their hometown team got driven into the ground. After a moment, Ben shrugged. “I guess we can go listen to his offer. But I want to make sure you’re not overworked the way you were before. You’ve been so much happier out from underneath that job. I don’t want to lose this.”

Rider brought Ben’s hand to his mouth. “We’ll do what’s best for us. No matter what he offers, it has to benefit our marriage above everything.”

Ben nodded.

Rider unmuted the call. “We’re on our way to the airport now.”

“Beautiful. I’ll have a car waiting when you land.”

Ben stared at Rider’s profile and prayed this wasn’t a mistake. But Ben trusted

Rider to always put them first. No matter what, they would be fine.

Tanner's private plane was nice as hell, but it nearly gave Rider anxiety just sitting inside. He had thought he was free of this. Rider weighed the pros and cons of getting sucked back into this life. Truthfully, the pros far outweighed the cons. Yet he still didn't know what he would do. He needed Ben to be happy. Secretly, the thing Tanner had said that got under his skin was the boredom comment. Rider could never tire of Ben, but maybe Ben would be restless without a challenge. Ben was twenty-nine to Rider's days away forty-two. Rider didn't want him to suddenly notice that gap one day when his mind got too settled. He wanted to keep Ben's focus forever.

"I used to watch you on these flights and daydream about fucking you."

Ben's sudden confession immediately pulled Rider from his worries. Rider glanced over, expecting to share a smile over the admission. Instead, he found Ben staring at him with so much hunger, it seared his skin. Rider's mouth went dry. Ben made him so goddamn hot. "You should've done it."

Some confidence left Ben's features. "I was certain someone like you could never want someone like me."

That confused the fuck out of Rider. "What do you mean? I used to watch you work and silently beg for you to turn your head and see how much I craved you." Rider stood and bent, boxing Ben in with hands on either side of Ben's head on the loveseat. "You'd chew your pen while focused on your tasks. I'd watch the way your lips moved and wish they were on me instead." Rider brushed his lips across Ben's mouth before moving away again. "You'd lean back in your chair and stretch. All I could do was picture being at your feet on my knees." Rider dropped to his knees.

Ben's eyes burned with lust as he watched Rider's every move. His expression made Rider feel powerful. He felt their ages disappear. Rider knew he would do things for Ben no one else would.

He slid Ben's zipper down while holding his stare. "You have no idea how hard I prayed you'd notice how completely in love I am with you. I have been for a very long time. If you had given me a single opening on any of these flights, I would've taken it like a champ with zero prep and no lube. There's no comparison between us." He popped Ben's erection from his shorts. "There's only a bigger love than anyone else could give either of us."

Rider held Ben's stare as he slowly leaned in and licked Ben's cock. "Tell me what you pictured doing to me."

Ben released a pant. "I pictured bending you over this loveseat, ensuring you never wanted anyone else again."

Rider held Ben's stare so he would see the truth. "I haven't wanted anyone else since the day we met. You were always meant for me." He went down on Ben, trying to drive home his words. Rider needed Ben to feel how desperate he had been since the first time Ben opened his mouth and put Rider in his place. He sucked. Ben whimpered. Rider swallowed. Ben's hips left the seat.

"I wrote you a letter once, telling you I love you, but I lost my nerve and shredded it."

Rider's head shot up at the confession. "Really?"

Ben looked desperate. He nodded. "It was the one and only time you threatened to fire me when it looked like you actually might. I didn't want to go without you knowing how I felt."

Rider didn't know when that happened. "I've never once meant it when I threatened to fire you. I can't live without you."

"Prove it." The way Ben growled the words nearly made Rider laugh. He wasn't trying to torment Ben, but it seemed he was.

"Yes, sir." He took Ben to the back of his throat.

"Damn. That feels so good."

Rider barely heard the words. He was too focused on giving Ben the blowjob of the year. The more sounds Ben made, the faster Rider bobbed. He didn't change angles or tease him. Rider wanted Ben's cum to hit the back of his throat. A strangled cry caressed his ears. Cum filled Rider's mouth.

"Oh my god. I love you. I love you so fucking much."

Rider swiped his face on his shoulder before moving to claim Ben's mouth. Their heated kiss cooled as Rider slowed things down. He didn't want some quick blowjob or whatever. Rider wanted to sit on Ben's dick. Unfortunately, he had ensured that would have to wait.

The crackle of the intercom cut through their moment. "We're starting our final descent. Please fasten your seatbelts."

Ben chuckled against his lips. "We cut that a little close. I'll have to make it up to you later."

That was Rider's plan. He helped Ben fix his clothes, and they buckled their seatbelts. As the plane landed smoothly, they snuggled until the motors died. They held hands on the way to the waiting SUV. On the drive, they kept casting lustful looks each other's way. Rider didn't know how they would make it through this trip. He hadn't gotten less than half mast since touching Ben's dick. His brain was more begging to get dicked down than any other thoughts. Rider needed to get it together before he agreed to something stupid with Tanner, just to get out of there faster.

The car circled a huge driveway in front of a massive house. Tanner's home was more like a compound. No one made it onto the property unless they were specifically invited and escorted. In his life,

Rider had interacted with many of the elite. Tanner was the only one so untouchable. His money meant everything to him. Rider had never been very good at dealing with him. Ben, who had never met anyone as rich before Tanner, handled the guy like a master.

Their driver opened their doors. Together, they climbed from the car. Rider took a steadying breath. He didn't want to do anything that might fuck up their beautiful life. Rider couldn't claim he didn't love the Chuckers, though. It hurt his chest to think of them failing without his backing. The front door opened as they climbed the steps. A butler stepped aside, quietly welcoming them inside.

He closed the door behind him. "Your presence is awaited in the front sitting room."

That was odd. They usually met in Tanner's home office. It seemed Tanner planned to try acting human as a tactic by meeting them like friends. Rider kissed Ben's hand as they headed for the front room. It was his way of drawing strength. Ben flashed him a reassuring smile. Another of Tanner's employees opened the door to the front room.

"Surprise!"

Rider startled and then froze. He eyed the room. He blinked at the sight of his mom, middle brother, and all the Chuckers' players and staff. "Um. What the fuck is this?"

Ben laughed. "It's a birthday party."

Rider looked his way. He was super slow on the uptake. It hit him Ben had known about this. "What?"

Ben rolled his eyes. "Your birthday is in two days. I got you. You should see your face." His eyes swam with laughter.

He absolutely had gotten Rider. No way in hell would he have thought a party awaited him at Tanner's.

"How did you do this?"

Ben shrugged. "I talked to Tanner when he called last month about us coming back to work. We got off track and agreed you should be celebrated for once. He handled everything."

Tanner stepped forward. He was all smiles. Rider didn't know what part shocked him the most, the party, the fact that Tanner had planned it, or that his family was there. Well, part of them. He didn't see Matt. That made him sad. Matt hadn't talked to him since he had walked out of Rider's office.

As a bear of a man, Tanner blocked out the rest of the guests as he greeted Rider. He patted Rider's back. His eyes were alight with laughter. "Happy birthday, son."

Rider shook his hand. He couldn't stay quiet. "This doesn't mean I accept your offer."

A loud guffaw of laughter burst from Tanner. "This isn't about that. I swear. You'd think you believe I don't like you. You've been with me for years, giving everything to my team. I consider Ben and you family."

"I'm pretty sure I told you to go fuck yourself the last time we spoke."

That made Tanner laugh harder. "See? If you didn't think of me as family too, you never would've felt comfortable saying that."

Honestly? Rider couldn't deny it. He spent entirely too many years and time with Tanner to ignore they had some form of relationship. Family seemed a bit far, though.

Jules rushed forward to hug him. "There's my eldest baby." She leaned close to his ear. "I thought Tanner was an old guy with one foot in the grave. Why didn't you tell me he's a sexy silver fox? Imagine all that money."

All Rider could do was shake his head. His mom was who she was. He had accepted it a long time ago. Rider got carried away by the tide of well-wishers.

Several players asked when he planned to return to the team. It seemed Tanner's talk of Medvedkov leaving wasn't just bullshitting him to get him there. Apparently, Tanner's second choice was a man well known for slashing pay and booting people back to the minors at the slightest bad run. None of them felt comfortable with the team any longer. Rider listened to their concerns through cake and ice cream. He got cards and gifts Ben gathered for him. His gaze kept moving Ben's way and lingering. As always, Ben quietly kept his life organized and made it easier. Rider had never stood a chance against loving him.

The first moment Rider had to talk to him, he pulled Ben aside. "You're amazing. I can't believe you did this. What would you have done if I had refused to come here?"

Ben shrugged. "I would've suggested we come hear Tanner out and you've would've agreed."

Rider couldn't argue with his logic. "I don't deserve you."

Ben shrugged. "You don't let me spoil you, but I want to. I had to do what I could."

"I love you."

Ben beamed. "I love you too."

Rider's smile faltered. "We have to return to the team."

A sweet smile touched Ben's lips. "I know." Ben's smile grew. "But we can make Tanner squirm and give us everything we want."

They held each other's stare. Rider had so much to say, he didn't know where to start. Ben had saved his life. He didn't realize it, but Rider had disappeared before him. There had been nothing left of him but the Chuckers' general manager. Then Ben had come along and reminded him he was also a man with feelings and needs. Desires. Rider never knew how to say all those things.

"Can you believe Mom thought Tanner was some elderly dude, wasting away up here in his compound?"

Ben snorted. "I might've gently led her to believe that."

A laugh burst from Rider. Happiness overshadowed everything inside him.

They were absolutely meant to be. Ben got him. He got Rider's family. Ben saw Rider's mom for the opportunist she was and kept her wrangled. No one else on this earth could have married him, stepped into his unique family, and survived. Ben had everything under control, including Rider. He never wanted to be anywhere else but under Ben's thumb... except maybe underneath him.

"How long do we have to stay?" Rider undressed Ben with his eyes, ensuring he understood Rider's impatience.

Ben licked his lips, obviously feeling the same. "This party is for you, so for a good while." He leaned Rider's way. "But I bet I can get you off in the bathroom before anyone even notices we're gone."

Rider whimpered. "God, I love you."

Ben's bright smile was everything. "I love you too."

As Ben took his hand and led him out of sight before anyone noticed, Rider couldn't stop smiling. He also couldn't stop thanking fate for handing him this amazing man. Rider absolutely couldn't live without him. He had no plans to ever try.

Don't forgct to check out the next Thin Ice, *Royally Pucked*.

About the Author

Charity Parkerson is an award-winning and multi-published author with several companies. Born with no filter from her brain to her mouth, she decided to take this odd quirk and insert it in her characters. One of her greatest loves is writing morally gray characters. You'll find them scattered throughout her hundreds of titles.

*Eight-time Readers' Favorite Award Winner

*2015 Passionate Plume Award Finalist

*2013 Reviewers' Choice Award Winner

*2012 ARRA Finalist for Favorite Paranormal Romance

*Five-time winner of The Mistress of the Darkpath

Connect with her online:

*Sign up for her newsletter: https://bit.ly/charityparkersonnewsletter

*Join her readers' group on Facebook: http://bit.ly/CharitysTribe

*Website: https://www.charityparkerson.com

*A list of her social media accounts and giveaways all in one place: http://hy.page/charityparkerson

www.ingramcontent.com/pod-product-compliance
Lightning Source LLC
LaVergne TN
LVHW010658110826
845149LV00014B/3143

* 9 7 8 1 9 5 9 5 7 6 3 8 9 *